RIDER WOOFSON

UNDERCOVER IN THE BOW-WOW CLUB

BY WALKER STYLES ● **ILLUSTRATED BY BEN WHITEHOUSE**

LITTLE SIMON

New York   London   Toronto   Sydney   New Delhi

LITTLE SIMON

An imprint of Simon & Schuster Children's Publishing Division
1230 Avenue of the Americas, New York, New York 10020
First Little Simon hardcover edition May 2016
Copyright © 2016 by Simon & Schuster, Inc.
Also available in a Little Simon paperback edition.

Designed by Laura Roode. The text of this book was set in ITC American Typewriter.
Manufactured in the United States of America 0416 FFG
2 4 6 8 10 9 7 5 3 1
This book has been cataloged with the Library of Congress.
978-1-4814-6304-1 (hc)
978-1-4814-6303-4 (pbk)
978-1-4814-6305-8 (eBook)

CONTENTS

THE AIR-DRUMMER

Click-click-click-click. Crash! Crash! Clatter! Rat-a-tat! Boom!

"What's with all the noise?!" asked a floppy-haired mutt named Ziggy Fluffenscruff. "I was having the most amazing dream about a thirty-foot-long super-sandwich—until the noise woke me. Can't a pup take a *catnap* in peace?"

"Sorry about that," said Westie. He was a brilliant West Highland terrier, and the P.I. Pack's inventor. "My latest creation can cause quite a commotion. I call it the Air-Drummer. It's half drum set, half ATV."

"I love TV!" Ziggy exclaimed, wagging his tail.

"Not a TV, kid," Rora Gooddog said, walking into the room. She was a poodle who was book smart and street smart. "An *ATV*. It stands for 'All-Terrain Vehicle.' That means it can travel anywhere."

"Well, can it go get me something to eat?" Ziggy said, rubbing his growling belly. "I'm hungry."

"Not so fast, fella,"

Rora said to Ziggy. Then she turned to Westie. "Mind if I give it a try?"

"Of course!" Westie said, offering her the driver's seat. "It still has a few kinks to work out, but given the right driver—"

Rora started playing the drum set. *Ba-da-da-ta-ba-tada-da!*

"You're amazing!" Westie said.

"You're totally a natural-born drummer dog!" Ziggy clapped.

"I'll dance to that!" said a stranger. He was a well-dressed whippet with fancy hair and a funky leather outfit.

"Bow-wowza!" Ziggy shouted, running in a circle around their cool-looking guest. "Mega-famous rock star, David Bow-Wowie! You're a music legend!"

"Calm down, team," said Rider Woofson, the finest dog detective in Pawston. He put his arm around the rock star. "Mr. Bow-Wowie is a close friend of mine, but today he's here on business."

"You know David Bow-Wowie?" Ziggy laughed. "But you don't know anything about music. "

"Not so," Bow-Wowie said. "Back in the day, Rider guarded some of the biggest names in music. Katy Purry. Three Dog Knights. Even Ma-dog-gona."

"You know Katy Purry?" Ziggy asked, wagging his tail.

Rider cleared his throat.

"Ahem, as I was saying, Bow-Wowie is here because there's a crime to be solved."

"We'll help in any way we can," Rora said, standing up. "What happened?"

Bow-Wowie looked both sad and

scared. "I came back to Pawston to play a benefit show to save the Bow-Wow Club. But all of my instruments have been stolen! By a ghost!"

"Ghastly!" Rora said.

"*Terrier*-fying!" Westie barked.

"G-G-G-Ghosts?!" Ziggy cried, covering his eyes with his paws.

"That's the *spirit*, team," Rider said. "Let's g-g-g-get g-g-g-ghostbustin'!"

MUSICAL GHOSTS

When the team arrived at the Bow-Wow Club, the police were guarding the entrance. Inside, the stage crew was hiding behind the seats. Everyone was frightened and whispering about spooky, toothy ghosts.

"'Spooky, toothy ghosts?'" Ziggy repeated.

"Before this place was the Bow-Wow Club, it was a dental office," Rora said. "Word on the street is that the Bow-Wow Club has been haunted by dentists."

"I don't like dentists," said Ziggy. "And I do not like *ghost* dentists."

"A clean mouth is a healthy mouth," Rider said. Ziggy stuck his tongue out at Rider behind his back. "And sticking your tongue out is rude."

"How'd you know I stuck my tongue out at you?!" Ziggy asked.

"Simple. I'm a good detective," Rider said with a wink.

"The best!" added Westie.

At the back door, there stood a familiar little dog. "Hello, Frenchie," Rider said. "I didn't know you worked here."

"Yeah, I just started guarding the door at the Bow-Wow Club. Free music and all the kibble I can eat. Pretty good deal. I can't believe what happened."

"Can you walk us through what you saw?" Rider asked.

"I can do better than that. I can show you the security video. Follow me." Frenchie led the P.I. Pack past the frightened crew. In the security office, Frenchie turned on a TV. An image of the

stage flashed to life, with two dogs setting up equipment. "The guys were unloading Mr. Bow-Wowie's instruments. That's Louis Labrador and Charlie Chihuahua."

The old stagehand in the video was a rough-looking labrador. He was working with a young, excited

chihuahua. Both of them were lift-
ing the precious instruments
from plastic crates.

"See this guitar here?"
Louis said. "It played the
solo on 'I Want To Hold
Your Paw'—only one
of the most famous
songs in history."

"Wow wow *wow!*"
Charlie said, making little jumps
in the air.

"And this," Louis said, holding up a microphone. "Bow-Wowie
sang into this when he recorded

the classic 'Smells like Dog Spirit.' "

"Wow wow wow *wow*!" Charlie said, jumping some more.

"And this is the keytar—"

"Wait, what's a keytar?" asked Charlie.

"It's half guitar, half keyboard," Louis explained. "It was used only

once, by the Rolling Bones, and then they gave it to Mr. Bow-Wowie as a gift."

"Wow wow wow wow *wow!*" Charlie said, jumping up and down even more. He was so excited, he looked like he might pass out. "What's this?" Charlie asked, pulling something from a crate.

"That is just a piece of Styrofoam," Louis said.

The dogs began to unload the

rest of the instruments. Charlie carefully put the drumsticks on the drum seat, but when he walked away, they fell off.

"Careful with those," Louis said.

"It wasn't me!" Charlie said. He put them back in place. He walked away, and the drumsticks fell again. But this time they started moving around on their own.

"Quit messing around," Louis said to Charlie.

"It's not me! I promise!" Charlie said. Suddenly, all of the instruments started moving on their own. Then they began marching around the stage.

"Ghosts! Ghosts! *G-G-Ghosts!*" Charlie shouted, leaping behind Louis. They both ran in circles and then hid behind a table. The instruments walked right out of the room.

"Instruments don't just walk around on their own," Rora said.

"But they just did," Westie noted. "We saw it on the video."

22

"Ghosts!" Ziggy barked.

"Don't believe everything you see on TV," Rider said. "It's time to sniff out some clues and find the real crook."

chapter
THREE

THE CAT'S MEOW

"My beloved instruments are . . . gone!" Bow-Wowie said as he walked in. He sat down on a crate, his heart broken. "The tambourine from 'The Cats in the Cradle,' the flute from 'Rumble in the Jungle,' the cello from 'Meow-low Yellow.' Oh, music is my life. Those instruments were like family. Without

them, I cannot make music—much less put on a show. I've lost my music *and* my favorite club!"

"Buck up, fella," Rora said. "The show ain't over until the *cat* lady sings."

"Then I must be hearing her *ssssong*," hissed Mr. Meow. The rich cat walked in with the mayor. They were good friends. Still, Rider found it odd that Mr. Meow always seemed to be nearby when bad news struck. "No mussssic benefit, no more Bow-Wow Club. And then I'm afraid I'll have to buy it."

"What are you talking about, fur ball?" Ziggy asked.

"Mr. Meow is right," the mayor said. "The Bow-Wow Club owes

money for its rent. If Mr. Bow-Wowie doesn't play, it will have to close, and the building will be up for sale."

"I plan to turn this place back into an office of dentistsssss," said Mr. Meow with a gleaming grin. "That will rid this city of thissss dreadful mussssic, and bring back some pearly white smilessss.

Good-bye, rock 'n' roll . . . hello,
clean gumsssss!"

"A boring old dental office is a
terrible idea," Ziggy said.

"It won't be boring or old," said Mr. Meow. "It will be the future of dentistry. Hundreds of dentistssss, scraping and cleaning and picking and—"

"Stop! Just thinking about it makes my teeth hurt." Ziggy moaned and held on to his mouth.

"Down, boy," Rider said to his young teammate. "Mr. Mayor, as much as I love dentists and a clean mouth, the Bow-Wow Club is an important part of Pawston. I'm going to get to the bottom of this mystery. How long do we have?"

"Only one day," the mayor said. "The concert was scheduled for tomorrow night. If enough money is made by then, Mr. Bow-Wowie can still save the club. If not . . ."

"What am I going to do?" Bow-Wowie groaned.

"It's not time to face the music just yet," Rider said. "I'm on the case, and I won't give up until I

find those instruments and the criminal that took them." Rider pulled his magnifying glass from the pocket of his trench coat. "Team, time to get to work."

"Besssst of luck," hissed Mr. Meow as he left with the mayor. "Call me when you fail, *sssso* I can tear down this stage."

"Bad kitty," Ziggy whispered.

"Mr. Meow may be rude, but he's still a citizen of Pawston, so he deserves our respect," Rider told the others. "Rest assured, we are going to keep the music alive in our fair city."

"That's a plan I can really dig," Rora said. "Let's look for clues."

The P.I. Pack started searching the club high and low. Bow-Wowie was beginning to worry again when all at once . . .

Rora said, "I found a clue!"

Westie said, "I found a clue too!"

Ziggy barked, "I found a clue three!"

"Make that four," Rider said.

chapter FOUR

OLD GOLD

"What have you got, team?" Rider asked.

"I was looking for the exits," Rora explained. "And there's a back door behind the stage that was open. I went outside and found these guitar strings next to a pair of tire tracks."

"Excellent work," Rider said.

"Westie, what did you find?"

"Using my Magnet-o-meter, I found a metal trapdoor on the other side of the stage," Westie said. "It leads to the basement."

"Great job. We'll search it after we hear from Ziggy," Rider noted.

"Uh . . . just a minute!" Ziggy's

head was stuck inside a picnic basket. He put his front paws on it and pushed as hard as he possibly could. When the basket flew off his head, an empty bottle of maple syrup fell out. "I found a maple-syrup bottle."

"Get real, kid," Rora said, her arms crossed. "I'd hardly call that a clue."

"But it is!" Ziggy said. "My gut says so."

"Isn't your gut usually just hungry?" Westie asked.

"Yeah, but—"

"Moving on," Rider interrupted. "I found something as well. It's not a clue, but I think it'll give our client a little hope." Rider pulled out a guitar from a small room.

"My best electric guitar!" Bow-Wowie shouted in glee. He jumped

up from his chair and hugged the
guitar close. "Why weren't you
stolen, my dear?"

"I had it," said Frenchie. The

shy security guard looked embarrassed. "But I promise I wasn't trying to steal it. You're my musical hero. I only wanted to clean it up nice and shiny for you. I was dusting it in my office when the other instruments walked away."

"Looks like your thoughtfulness paid off," Rider said.

As Bow-Wowie strummed his guitar, the detectives headed into the basement. Rider turned on the lights so they could see. As they looked around the room, there was nothing but old dental chairs and

equipment covered in spider webs.
In one corner, there was a large
anthill. The tiny red ants moved
around quietly.

"Ewww, this place gives me the
shivers!" Westie said.

"It wasn't so bad," Bow-Wowie
said. "My grandfather was a dentist and used to own this place.

WHIPPET & WHIPPET, DENTIST & SONS

He named it "Whippet & Whippet, Dentist & Sons." My father was a dentist like his father. He wanted me to become one too. But I didn't care about teeth. All I cared about was my music."

"What happened to the dental office?" Rora asked.

"My uncle worked here too, which was funny because he had a sweet tooth. He always carried around a bottle of maple syrup in his pocket because he ate it all the time. One night, he was working

late and lost a shipment of gold. He said ghosts took it."

"G-G-G-Gold?" Ziggy said, his ears perking up.

"Back then, they used *gold* to fill cavities. If a patient lost a tooth, they'd give them a new gold tooth," Bow-Wowie explained. "After the gold

disappeared, my uncle sold the place. Years later, it turned into the Bow-Wow Club."

"But what happened to the gold?!" Ziggy asked, his tail wagging.

"No one ever found it. Treasure hunters tried, but it's still missing. In fact, those gold-diggers started saying that this place was haunted too. They claimed to see things

moving around on their own. I never believed it . . . until now."

"That is a rather interesting tall *tail*," Rider said, "but we need to focus on the musical instruments. Let's solve one mystery at a time. Looks like we need to follow our next clue: the tire tracks."

As Rider led the team outside, Ziggy stayed behind. He was looking at some pictures on the wall. One was of Bow-Wowie's father, grandfather, and uncle.

"You coming, Zig?" Rider asked.

"In a minute," Ziggy said, sniffing around. He couldn't help but feel like they were missing something. He just didn't know what.

chapter
FIVE

THE TRAIL ENDS HERE

"What now?" Rora asked.

"I am scanning the tire tracks into my Foll-o-matic," Westie said. "It will record the marks and follow them to the getaway car."

The invention pointed down the road. "Good work, Westie," Rider said. "Now let's go track down those tire tracks."

"I hope we can help Mr. Bow-Wowie save the Bow-Wow Club," Rora said.

"So do I," agreed Rider. "He is a great musician, and Pawston deserves great music."

"Don't you think it's strange that Mr. Meow wants to open a dental office?" Ziggy asked as the Pack jumped into the van. "There are already plenty of other dentists in town."

"Mr. Meow is a very rich man," Rider said. "He owns many stores in Pawston. But for some people,

nothing is ever enough. They just want more, more, more."

"More, more, more," Bow-Wowie mumbled from the way back seat as he scribbled on a little pad of paper.

"What are you doing?" Rora asked.

"Writing down song lyric ideas," he said.

"How can anyone write songs at a time like this?" Ziggy asked, scratching his head.

Bow-Wowie kept humming a tune and wrote more words in his notebook.

"The tracks lead here!" Westie
exclaimed after a few miles. He
pointed to a van parked in front of
a music store called MOE & WALLY'S
MUSIC WAREHOUSE.

"A music warehouse—it's the

perfect place to hide instruments!"
Rider said. "We're dealing with a
diabolical mind!"

The group jumped out of the
van and ran inside, and Rider
shouted, "Everyone, freeze!"

A tiny mole and a giant walrus

stood still and looked confused.

Rora pulled out several photographs of the stolen property. "Have you seen these instruments?"

Moe the mole squinted, then shrugged. "To be honest, I don't see very well."

Wally the walrus looked at the photos and said, "They're quite nice. I'm afraid they're far too nice for our store. Are you buying or selling them?"

"Neither," Rider said. "We're looking for the stolen property of—"

"Ohhh. Myyy. Goodness." Wally clapped his flippers together and started squealing. "Moe! Moe! You have to see this! It's David Bow-Wowie!"

"Yeah, right," said Moe, who couldn't see a thing.

"I think it's obvious these two are *not* criminal masterminds," Rora whispered to the others. They nodded in agreement.

"My poor instruments aren't here," Bow-Wowie said, holding his only guitar close. "This is hopeless."

Rider paused. The great detective was out of clues, but he didn't want to worry his old friend.

"Perhaps a tune will make him feel better," Westie said to Ziggy. Ziggy took down an

acoustic guitar from the wall and began to play. Westie joined him on the piano.

"I knew all my detectives were talented, but I didn't know you could each play music," Rider said.

"Of course," Ziggy said. "Music class was my favorite subject

in school. Probably because my teacher gave us treats."

"This gives me an idea . . . ," Rider said, rubbing his paws together. "David, can you play the show tomorrow night with only one guitar? I have what the kids call a groovy plan."

chapter
SIX

THE CONCERT
OF CHAOS

"It looks like a *zoo* out there!" Ziggy gulped. He peeked out at the audience from behind the curtain. Rora and Westie looked over his shoulder. They gulped too.

"I don't know if I can do this without all of my instruments," Bow-Wowie said.

"That's why we're here," Rider

said, patting his friend on the back.
You play your guitar. Westie will
play the piano and keytar. Ziggy
will play bass. And Rora is going
to bring the beat with Westie's
very special drum set."

"Where will you be?"

"Next to you," Rider said, "playing the electric guitar that Moe and Wally let me borrow."

"Boss, remind me why we are playing a concert when we *should* be solving a crime," Rora said.

"Because we're going to do

both at the same time," Rider said. "Criminals always return to the scene of the crime when they didn't finish the job."

"I get it," Rora said with a nod. "You mean, whoever stole the other instruments probably wanted the whole set. Once they see Bow-Wowie up onstage with his famous guitar, they'll make a grab for it."

"Exactly," Rider said.

"You're using my last guitar as bait?!" the rock star whined. "Isn't there some other worm we can use to fish with?"

"You have to trust me," Rider said. "Now let's go out there and raise the *ruff*!"

As soon as the band took

the stage, the crowd went wild. Everyone began shouting and whistling.

Front row and center was Rotten Ruffhouse, the evil rottweiler crook. And he was staring right at Bow-Wowie. "Looks like you were right!" Rora yelled, winking at Rider. The thief had returned to the scene of the crime.

The group kept playing. They were waiting for Rotten to make his move. Instead, he was . . . dancing?

The band was halfway through

the show when Bow-Wowie started singing his most famous song, "Black Cat." That's when Rotten jumped on the stage and ran toward Bow-Wowie. But he didn't try to snatch the guitar. Instead, he started singing into the micro- phone like he was the lead singer.

The P.I. Pack was completely confused, but they needed to stop the criminal. "Catch that singing

suspect, P.I. Pack!" Rider shouted.

Rotten saw the detectives and dove off the stage into the crowd. The audience went wild. They

passed him hand to hand, letting him crowd-surf to the back of the room. "He's escaping!" Ziggy cried.

"No, he's not!" Rora said. She pressed a button on the Air-Drummer and started playing even harder. As she beat the drums,

the cymbals began spinning and
the ATV–drum set hovered off the
stage. The Air-Drummer was part
helicopter, and Rora flew it after
Rotten!

chapter SEVEN

A NOISY CHASE

"Are you slowpokes coming?" Rora shouted over the rat-a-tat drumming. Rider and Westie tossed their microphone cables up, latching onto the drum set. As the three flew over the crowd, the audience cheered even louder, thinking this was all part of the show!

Rotten looked back to see the

detectives and ran out of the Bow-Wow Club. Rora kept beating the drums to chase after him. She barely made it under the door as Westie and Rider climbed onto the sides of the Air-Drummer.

"Nice drumming, Rora!" Rider said.

"Nice *flying*, Rora!" Westie said.

"Thanks, boys!" Rora blasted outside over the street traffic and after Rotten. Everyone stared at the music-making whirlybird. "Stop, you pesky mutt!"

"I told you I'm a rottweiler!"

Rotten shouted back. The punk pooch leaped over cars and cabs. The Air-Drummer twirled and turned quickly to chase him.

Rotten jumped over a fence and turned down an alley, but it was a dead end. He had nowhere to go.

The Air-Drummer was in hot pursuit as Rora played even harder. The beating of the drums was louder than ever.

An old parakeet came to his window and shouted, "Keep it down out there, you young whippersnappers. I'm trying to sleep!" Then the old bird threw a rolled-up newspaper. It hit the off button on the Air-Drummer.

"Uh-oh!" Westie said.

The drum set fell out of the sky and landed on Rotten. "I give up," he said, waving his hand.

Rider pulled the criminal out from under the Air-Drummer.

"You have the right to remain silent—" Rora started.

"Silent about what?" Rotten said. "I didn't do anything. The only thing I am guilty of is seeing my favorite rock star in concert."

"But you ran onstage!" Westie said.

"Of course I did. I have a VIP pass!" Rotten said. He held up a badge that read: VERY IMPORTANT PUP. "I won it on the radio for correctly answering twenty-five trivia questions about David Bow-Wowie. I'm his biggest fan."

"Is that why you stole his instruments?" Rora asked.

"What?!" Rotten barked. "I would never steal his instruments. Let me go back to the concert with you, and I'll help however I can."

Rider scratched his head. If Rotten Ruffhouse was innocent, then this was turning into a real mystery.

chapter
EIGHT

THE GHOST STRIKES AGAIN

When the three detectives and Rotten returned to the concert, Bow-Wowie was still onstage playing a solo. The crowd was hypnotized by the music. Even Rotten Ruffhouse started to tear up.

"Are you crying?" Westie asked. "I thought you were a tough dog."

"I am," Rotten said, wiping a

tear from his snout. "But Bow-
Wowie's music is just so . . .
bow-wow-*wow*."

"Thank you! Thank you!" the
rock star shouted to the crowd
before running offstage. Rotten

and the detectives were there to meet him.

"Mr. Bow-Wowie, it's an honor," Rotten said. He kneeled down before the rock star.

"Are you the thief?" Bow-Wowie asked.

"I'm afraid not," Rider said. "He's your biggest fan."

Suddenly, gasps filled the concert hall. The Pack ran to see what was happening. The lights were flashing and Bow-Wowie's favorite guitar was moving around on stage . . . on its own.

"It must be the ghost!" someone

yelled. The crowd exited safely out of the Bow-Wow Club as fast as they could.

"After that guitar!" shouted Rider. But the lights shut off. When they came on again, the last guitar was gone.

"Nooooooooooooo!"
David Bow-Wowie fell
to his knees. "All of
my dear instruments
are gone! I'll never
play music again!"

"Nooooooooooooo!"
Rotten Ruffhouse fell
to his knees. "All
of my dear songs
are gone! I'll never
hear them again!"

"Did you see that?"
Westie cried. "G-G-G-Ghosts *are*
real!" He tucked his tail between

his legs and hid behind his friends.

Rider and Rora were stumped. "I've never had a case I couldn't solve," Rider said.

"Wait a minute," Rora said. "Where's Ziggy?"

"Right here," Ziggy said as he poked his head up from the metal trap door to the basement. "And don't worry. I have all the *ant*-swers."

chapter
NINE

THE WHOLE TOOTH AND NOTHING BUT THE TOOTH

"Well, spit it out already, kid!" Rora barked. "Who's the thief?"

"Not thief," Ziggy said. "*Thieves*. As in more than one. I suspected they might strike again, so I stayed behind while all of you chased Rotten."

"How did you know Rotten was innocent?" Rider asked.

"I saw his VIP badge when Frenchie let him up onstage."

"Is this the part with the ghosts?" Westie asked nervously.

"There are no ghosts haunting here," Ziggy said.

"Then who made the lights flash and then turn off?" Rora asked.

"That was part of the show,"

Ziggy said. "It's all automatic."

"But the instruments moved on their own!" said Westie.

"No, they were actually moved by the thieves—only the thieves were too small to be seen."

"What are you talking about, kid?" Rora said. "This is a *flea*-brained idea."

"Not fleas," Ziggy said as he borrowed Rider's magnifying glass. Everyone could see a trail of tiny black ants moving

along the floor. "Ants follow each other based on a scent they make. This way they can search for food and still find their way back home. When we were first here, I could smell maple syrup everywhere. I thought that I was just hungry like always until I heard

Mr. Bow-Wowie's story about his uncle."

"But my uncle hasn't been here for years. He moved to New Yorkie City and started his own maple syrup company."

"Your uncle may not be here anymore, but the ants have always been here," said Ziggy. "They stole your instruments and something else I think you'll want. Follow me so I can show you the good news."

"I hope there's no bad news." Bow-Wowie frowned.

Ziggy led everyone into the basement. "There's no bad news, Mr. Bow-Wowie, but there is better news: I know how to save the Bow-Wow Club forever."

Ziggy walked into the middle of the room and pulled up the old floorboards. Underneath were all of Bow-Wowie's instruments!

"My dear instruments are saved!" Bow-Wowie sang out. "I will play all of you every day for the rest of my life!"

"My music is saved!" Rotten cried out. "I will come to all of your

shows for the rest of my life!"

Westie gave a sheepish laugh. "See . . . I *knew* there was no such thing as ghosts."

"Sure you did," Ziggy said with a smirk. "Looks like the mystery is solved."

"Not quite, kid," Rora said.

"Why did the ants take the instruments?"

"I can answer that one," Rotten said. "David Bow-Wowie is a very superstitious rock star. He puts a few dabs of syrup on all of his instruments before a show!"

Bow-Wowie nodded that this was true.

"Why would you do that?" Rora asked.

"You see, my uncle loved syrup," Bow-Wowie explained. "And my uncle is the only one who told me to follow what I love too. Everyone else told me to be a dentist. But my uncle understood me. He loved syrup, and I loved playing music. So I add syrup to my instruments for good luck."

"And the ants found the syrup and took the instruments back to their home," Westie concluded.

"I should have trusted your gut, Ziggy," Rider said.

"And your nose. But what's this about saving the club?"

"Oh yeah," Ziggy said. He pulled

back the rest of the floorboards. There were hundreds of chunks of gold.

"*Bow-wowza!* It's the old missing gold!" Bow-Wowie yelled with joy.

"*Bow-wowza*, indeed," Ziggy said. "After following the ants and the smell of maple syrup down here,

I began to wonder. If the ants love syrup enough to steal instruments, they probably love syrup enough to steal gold, too."

Ziggy took down a framed picture from the wall. "I'll bet your uncle had sticky fingers. They were probably covered in syrup all the time. If he touched that gold, then the gold was covered in syrup, so the ants stole that, too."

"You did it, kid," Rora said. "You solved two mysteries with one solution."

"I'm proud of ya, Zig," Rider said.

"I am in your debt," Bow-Wowie said. "You saved my instruments and the Bow-Wow Club. How can I ever repay you?"

"Ever hear of a thirty-foot-long super-sandwich?" Ziggy said with a grin.

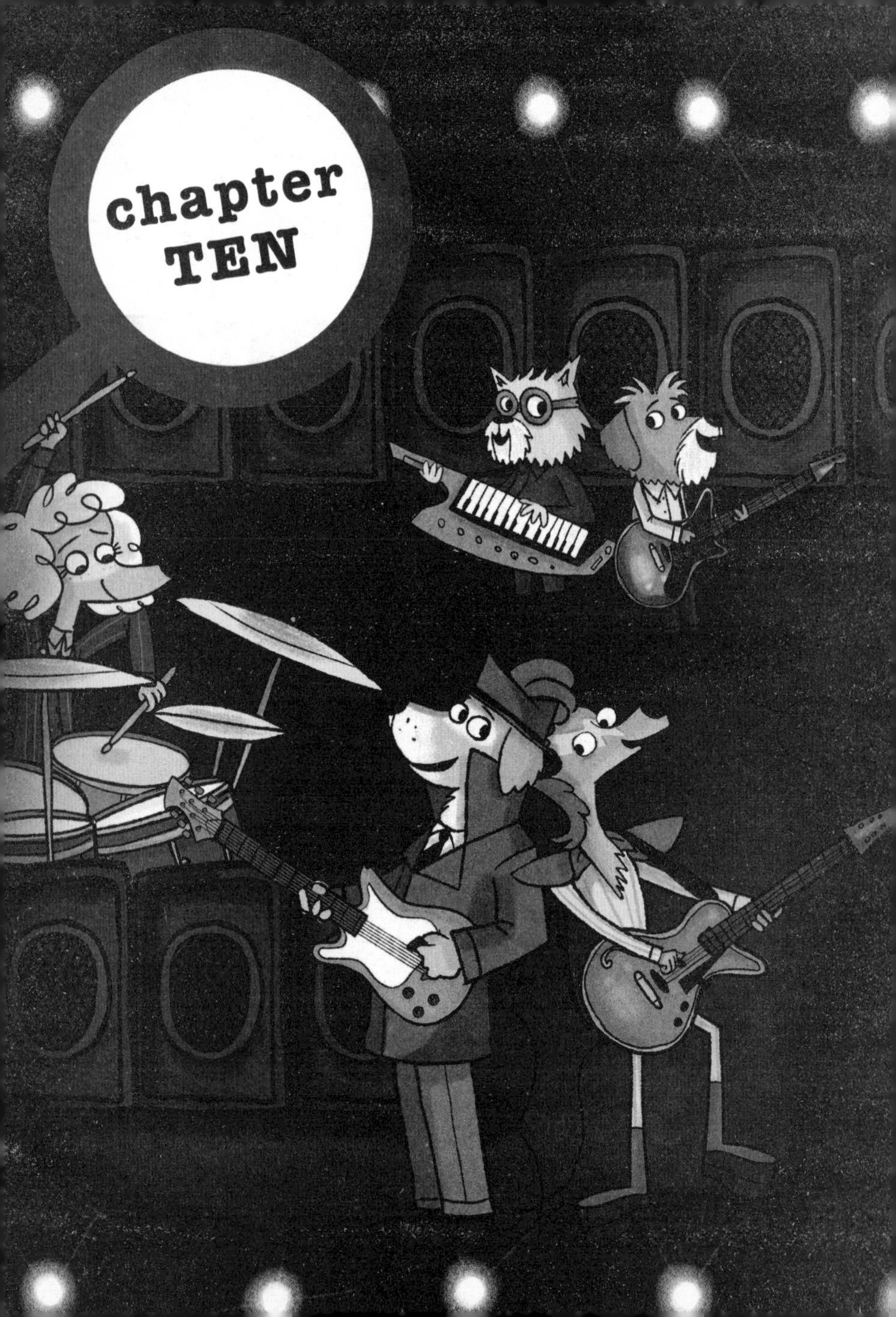
chapter
TEN

A LONG HISS GOOD NIGHT

After the great discovery, David Bow-Wowie used the gold to pay the bank. Then he invited his fans back to the club for a second free concert. He played music all night to celebrate the Bow-Wow Club staying open. For a special song, the rock star asked the P.I. Pack to join him on the stage. Bow-Wowie spoke into the microphone. "I'd like to give thanks to one of my oldest friends—the greatest detective in Pawston—Rider Woofson!"

The crowd cheered.

"I'd also like to thank my new friends, with an extra special shout out to the pup who saved the day—Ziggy Fluffenscruff!" The crowd cheered again.

"But someone *special* gets a little extra love from me tonight. . . ."

Both Rora and Rotten Ruffhouse perked up their ears.

"My instruments! The best friends a musician can have!" The rock star hugged his guitar close. Rora and Rotten frowned.

Across the street, in a tall building, a cat stood in the window. He began hissing at the moon. He even slammed his paw onto his windowsill in anger. "I wassss ssssso closssse!"

Mr. Meow turned away and hissed some more. "I ussssed maple ssssyrup to lead those antssss to thossssessssticky instrumentsssss. Rotten kept going on and on about Bow-Wowie's foolish ssssuperstition. It would have been the perfect crime, if not for that mutt detective and his smelly sidekickssss! One of thessssse dayssss, Rider

Woofsssson, I will have my revenge."

The wicked cat looked down at the Bow-Wow Club. But no one noticed him as the wonderful music blared into the street and everybody danced.

CHECK OUT RIDER WOOFSON'S NEXT CASE!

"Kee-yah!"

The Pawston Martial Arts Dojo was filled with animals practicing their best moves. At the front of the class was Westie Barker, a brilliant terrier with a mind for science. Lately, he was trying to learn the fighting style of Bark-Jitsu.

Excerpt from *Ghosts and Goblins and Ninja, Oh My!*

"Kee-yah!" Westie shouted again as he hit a plank of wood, but it didn't break.

"You've got this!" the P.I. Pack shouted from the front row. They were sitting with the friends and family of the entire class.

"I hope Westie gets his yellow belt this time around," said Rora Gooddog, the smartest dame in the P.I. game.

"Me too," said Rider Woofson. Rider was the team leader and the best dog detective in Pawston City. "Westie's been working very hard."

Excerpt from *Ghosts and Goblins and Ninja, Oh My!*

"Can you believe all the snacks here are healthy?!" barked Ziggy Fluffenscruff, the youngest member of the team. "They don't have candy or potato chips or anything tasty."

"Do you always think with your stomach, kid?" Rora asked.

"If my tummy is a-rumbling, then I'm a-grumbling," Ziggy replied with a smirk.

"Silence in the dojo, please," said Sensei Hiro. "Today, our students will begin to learn the secrets of Bark-Jitsu."

Excerpt from *Ghosts and Goblins and Ninja, Oh My!*